I AM MY HAIR

Kinyel Friday

Illustrations by Robert Roberson Jr.

HEY!

I'm Tanya!

I'm super excited
to go to
school today!

I have been counting down the days since the summer.

New school.
New clothes.
New backpack.
New hairstyle.

And I'm all set to start my new journey!

After breakfast, my parents, my older brother Charles, and I hop into my dad's car and head to school. **FINALLY!**

We walk into the school to meet my teacher, Ms. Davis. We've already taken a tour of the school and met Principal Johnson, but the school looks bigger with all of the other kids and parents there too.

Most of all, I'm giddy about meeting some new friends. I quickly kiss my parents good-bye, hug Charles, and run off to play.

I join a group of girls who are playing with my favorite toys-- dolls.

We talk.
We laugh.
We play.
We pretend.

All of a sudden, one of the girls stops playing and touches my afro puffs. She says, "Hey, your hair is weird. It feels like a sheep." The other friend says, "Baa!" My two new "friends" laugh.

Tears fill my eyes. "STOP!"
I run away from the group,
put my head down on the
table furthest away from the
mean girls, and cry.
I am so hurt.

Ms. Davis walks over to me with some tissues. I describe what happened through my sniffles. "I'm so sorry that happened to you, Tanya." Ms. Davis gives me a hug and calls the mean girls over.

We talk about my feelings and how it is not okay to touch someone without asking. Bullying behaviors, such as laughing at others and making fun of other folks, are not okay choices. There is a lesson to be learned for everyone in the group.

Each of the girls say, "I'm sorry" and gives me a hug. For the rest of play time, the group each draws an apology note and gives them to me before we begin class.

During recess, Ms. Davis writes my parents a note about what happened. When I get home, I show my parents the note and we sit down to have a family meeting.

"Why am I so different," I ask.

"Let me tell you about your hair," Mom says. She takes me to the bathroom mirror.
"You *are* your hair. You know why?"
"Why" Tanya asks.

You are
BEAUTIFUL

You are
SOPHISTICATED

You are
UNIQUE

You are
HEALTHY

You are
DARING

You are
STRONG

You are
AMAZING

You are
SWEET

You are
PRECIOUS

You are

IMAGINATIVE

You are
SOFT & CUDDLY

You are
SPUNKY

You are
STYLISH

"Don't ever let anyone make you feel ashamed of your hair. It's something that makes you even more beautiful and even more

It would be boring if everyone looked the same." Dad kisses me on top of my head.

I giggle and strike some poses.
"I love my hair and I love me!
AND, I think I want some braids
tomorrow, PLEASE!"

To my family, thank you for your support. I love you. To girls of color, you are beautiful and don't let anyone tell you different. —K.F.

Foremost, thanks to God. To the family and friends who inspire and encourage me, much love. —Robert